Nantucket Sextant

Mary Keating

outskirts press

Nantucket Sextant
All Rights Reserved.
Copyright © 2024 Mary Keating
v3.0

This is a work of fiction. Names, characters, businesses, places, events, locales, and incidents are either the products of the author's imagination or used in a fictitious manner. Any resemblance to actual persons, living or dead, or actual events is purely coincidental.

The opinions expressed in this manuscript are solely the opinions of the author and do not represent the opinions or thoughts of the publisher. The author has represented and warranted full ownership and/or legal right to publish all the materials in this book.

This book may not be reproduced, transmitted, or stored in whole or in part by any means, including graphic, electronic, or mechanical without the express written consent of the publisher except in the case of brief quotations embodied in critical articles and reviews.

Outskirts Press, Inc.
http://www.outskirtspress.com

ISBN: 978-1-9772-7170-9

Cover Photo by Stirling Martin © 2024 istockphoto.com. All rights reserved - used with permission.

Outskirts Press and the "OP" logo are trademarks belonging to Outskirts Press, Inc.

PRINTED IN THE UNITED STATES OF AMERICA

To those who inspired

Annie Dillard, Virginia Woolf, James Joyce

And

to my favorite island

Nantucket

Write as if you were dying…
what would you begin writing if you
knew you would die soon?

Annie Dillard

Introduction

The Quakers first put their faith in the Holy Spirit, not God or in Jesus Christ. The Holy Spirit was the spirit of Truth.

It is 1702 and a visiting minister is coming to Nantucket. Mary Coffin Starbuck will hold the meeting in her home, known as Parliament House. The preacher is a Quaker. A soft wind of change is blowing toward Nantucket and many Quakers have visited over the last twenty years. Almost everyone has been to a Meeting. They all know it begins with a period of silence. The quiet ripples outward through the windows to the crowd standing in the yard. After a few minutes the shifting in their seats calms down. The preacher suggests that the world could be a much better place. His main listener is Mary Coffin Starbuck. She is moved to tears. Mary

Coffin Starbuck is the island's chief creditor in her store and few items leave or arrive on the island without passing through her hands. When she weeps the congregation sobs. They are moved to tears by the minister's eloquent words and vision.

The Friends, without the 'fire and brimstone' of Puritan beliefs in England and Massachusetts become the main religion on Nantucket. They believe in peace, honesty, and love. This, says Mary Coffin Starbuck, is the "overwhelming Truth."

When a French writer, Crevecoeur visited Nantucket in the eighteenth century he couldn't believe the non-violence he saw. In his journal, he wrote: "The Friends compose two-thirds of the magistracy of the island …..In all this apparatus of the law, its coercive powers are seldom wanted or required. No man has lost his life here judicially since the foundations of the town, no gibbets loaded with guilty citizens offer themselves to your view, no soldiers are appointed to bayonet their compatriots into servile compliance. How?"

And what struck Crevecoeur even more was how the women handled the business of the place: “To this dexterity in managing their husband’s business whilst he is absent the Nantucket wives united a great deal of industry…The men cheerfully give their consent to every transaction that has happened during their absence and all is joy and peace. However, the absence of men disposes the women to go to each other’s homes which consists of a social chat, a cup of tea, and ever hearty supper. As inebriation is unknown, and music and dancing are held in abhorrence, they could never fill all the vacant hours of their lives without the repast of the table.”

Tonight, in the twenty-first century, darkness comes early to Nantucket. No one seems to mind because everyone’s thoughts anticipate the Christmas Stroll. It is Nantucket’s fifth decade of the stroll and the most festive time of the year, second only to summer, so the ferries are making extra crossings. Nantucket has an air of excitement and wonder under the dark December skies filled with beautiful bright constellations.

Molly: Nurse

It wasn't that she was an islander at all. She had only spent a few summers there in her youth and made a few vacation trips with her Mother over the years; the last one she remembers vividly because her Mother had Alzheimer's. Now she was packing to return. Not that her life could ever be permanently on Nantucket as it was far far too expensive to even rent a home. Even the affordable sweet inns of the 20th century had been renovated and brought into the 21st century with prices increasing.

Nantucket had come full circle with its wealth. The Quakers were rich and the present-day homeowners were very rich. The difference being the Quakers did not flaunt their millions like Nantucket homeowners did now. All of this came up in Molly's mind but she didn't care tonight. She was going to venture out from her known self and arrive on the far-away island in the Atlantic because nowhere else would feel more comforting. She was sure of it.

Just nine months ago she managed to do the dumbest thing in her life. She had felt dizzy her shoulder ached and her heart was throbbing. None of her medical conditions required a call to a friend or so she thought.

It is late for Molly to be out, around 10 p.m. when she steps on the gas pedal and drives the old road that goes up and down around corners filled with shadowy trees. She prays she does not hit a deer. She didn't even dress with a hat and boots and scarf and gloves just ran out of the house without thinking. In a nightgown with flip flops and a cotton sweater in March. Flip flops. She had to get herself to the hospital. Who was she going to call and who could get to her as fast as she could drive herself? Luckily no one is around in Newburyport, Massachusetts to see this outfit. One does not drive on icy roads in March in Massachusetts when the snow and ice and wind can freeze you into the statue standing in the town square. There are few street lights on the country road to the hospital and the last one Molly saw was casting a yellow glow and then she saw nothing.

It was what she heard. A loud crash! Pitch black crash with ice and tree and embankment and steel crumbling. Shards of glass flying like snowflakes with sharp crystal points. A slump and a bang on the head over the steering wheel. Total blackness. No sound. Unconscious. She wakes to the sound of sirens. A flashlight pokes into her face. Molly's head is spinning. She is frightened…gurney…IVs, blood pressure, stitches, CAT scan.

She remembers being out of time. Light streams in her brain. A light she cannot identify separates her from her body. When she wakes a pain begins to creep into the body cells and her brain cannot make two plus two equal four. They ask her questions. What is your name. What day is it?

Molly Callahan. She isn't sure.

She sees a summer day on Nantucket. There are beach roses all over the cottages in S'conset.

She took her husband there once before he died of colon cancer. She made a bargain with herself, the kind people do when someone they love is dying.

She would stop working if he could only get better and they would go back to Colorado where he was happiest. But that bargain didn't work he died soon after her trip to S'conset on Nantucket.

Beach ros—es. Molly slurs out.

They sew ten stitches over her lip. She has a fractured rib and bruises all over her body. She takes a Selfie and sends it to her friends in the book club. She will be in the hospital two weeks then over to rehab for physical therapy. Molly's back hurts. She can't believe the black and blues puffed all over her face.

Oh, how she wishes she'd stayed home and dealt with her dizziness with some ice on her head. This is not my time to die, Molly tells herself. She always goes back to the Indian fortuneteller's words: "*They'll have to take you out and shoot you, you're going to live so long.*"

Molly closes her eyes to shut out the reality of where she is. When she opens her eyes again she makes a promise to herself.

When I get out of here...just one gift to myself. One time to the Christmas Stroll on Nantucket where I have never been. God damn it!

Molly checks her cell phone. There is a message back. Her son tells her to *hang in, Mom.*

Her son, Neil, in northern California, grows marijuana and loves his life out there. She remembers when she told him *not to walk out the door or he could just not come back.* He walked right out and never looked back at her.

What happened to me? What happens to everyone? Molly thought she was going to be with John her whole life. Not living here in a beautiful New England town on the coast in a small townhouse. She and John always walked the beach. He loved finding horseshoe crabs molting in the seaweed. Molly thought he would have made a good marine biologist. But he was a good history teacher. It just got to him at times. And often she would get a call from one of his drinking buddies at the bar saying John was drunk. Did he pick up a floozy once in awhile? She knew he did. Though he never brought her home. They only had to tousle their long blond hair at him over a bourbon and he was a goner. The floozy would take him back to her crummy little apartment in the next town over.

Why does she bother to save painful memories? They say the brain will do that: look at the painful much more often than the joy. So after twenty-seven years she has a dead husband and a son in California growing weed. And she has chosen to stop working in the healthcare field as a nurse. She is burned out.

She gave up her beautiful old home in Charlestown where she was a member of the community garden. She loved living there after her marriage. John taught at the community college and Molly worked at the High Street Bunker Hill Clinic. She met with friends once a month at the tavern for her book club. The tavern was her escape place.

Charlestown was a fashionable place to live in the 1800s and now it was having a resurgence of popularity because her friend Charles Rivers had renovated five historic buildings set for the wrecking ball. He was the project manager for the whole renovation project and now owned it. He was charming and often walked through the dining rooms of the tavern chatting with his customers. No one had believed in derelict buildings coming to life again.

But he made it happen. The town rediscovered its pride after losing it in mob wars, bank robberies, murders, and car thefts.

Molly and John moved into town just as it was rediscovered. Molly never worried about walking home to Sullivan Street after dark. She and John bought a three-decker home and renovated it.

Molly met Charles Rivers on one of those wintery afternoons when the kitchen closed for a few hours before dinner. Charles told Molly they'd all be welcome to come in for their book club meetings. Molly enjoyed drinking martinis then and loved that Charles flirted with her even though she was married.

It was the best bar in Boston. So much charisma from one end of the bar to the other. There was even a tavern tie that came in blue, green and maroon. Molly bought one for John at Christmas but he never wore it. College professors, lawyers, waiters and waitresses, cab drivers, politicians all downed a few after work. A piano player sat in the corner on weekends and belted out old favorites.

They were happy in Charlestown even though John often threatened to leave his teaching job and join the Merchant Marines. A blue-collar life appealed to his Jack London persona. Then the cancer came. Molly lost touch with many of her friends and once John took disability leave they left Charlestown for Newburyport.

Molly visited the community garden one last time. The garden had given her sustenance through the seven years she planted and weeded and smelled the sweet fragrant earth. Her sunflowers were her prize. They grew taller than she stood. Matty, the Irishman who tended the garden and ran it for the community was leaving for Oneonta, New York. Molly couldn't believe how this wave of loss had happened all at once. Leaving the book club, the garden with her friend, Matty and her husband diagnosed with cancer. Now she heard that even Charles Rivers was leaving town.

What would she do without her book club friends? The book club was planning a trip to Malaga next year. Molly leaned toward Algarve in Portugal but she hadn't been able to convince them to change their minds.

The weather was beautiful on the day Molly left the

hospital, one of those early spring days that bursts through in mid-March, when you know crocuses will soon be pushing up from the earth.

That night she couldn’t sleep. She went to the kitchen for something to eat and poured herself a glass of wine and then another.

Taking John to S'conset didn't cure him of his colon cancer. She wasn't sure who she had done it for, herself or John. He was an outdoors man, loved to hike and camp in Colorado and Maine. A real LL Bean kind of guy. He took Molly all the way up to the top of Mt. Katahdin way before it was the ‘in’ thing to do, way before they had routes and shelters and guides and workshops offering photography on the way up. So there she was, 5,269 feet up on the ‘Great Mountain’ Mt. Katahdin named by the Penobscot Indians. John told her to place a small stone on the peak. He didn’t say two words the whole trek back to base camp.

Did she feel exaltation the way she knew John felt rapture about climbing? It was later in the base camp inside the tent that they rolled and loved and probably made their baby Neil that night. Rolling on the earth smelling the pine knowing he would cook breakfast and make fresh coffee in the morning over an open fire under the sleeping bags all night searching out each other's body parts once twice "*Three times a lady*" that was his favorite song. She couldn't remember who sang it.

Molly's plan today which she will write on a post-it so she'll remember: *go to Christmas Stroll on Nantucket in December.* Find fun and maybe meet some guy at the Chicken Box and maybe have a dance again and drink till the sun comes up. She'll be in the place on earth she loves the best.

Molly poured another glass of wine. She especially remembers the fall she took her Mother to Nantucket for the cranberry festival, the year before her Mother died of Alzheimer's. They walked Main Street and bought sunflowers and gourds at the farmers' market to keep in their inn room. They rode the bus out to S'conset. That year the cranberry harvest was perfect and the sun gave it a galactic light of color she had never seen before.

Her Mother loved the island and kept repeating the same words over and over.

'Pretty.' 'Pretty.' She even said 'Pretty' when they walked below the dunes at S'conset. When they entered the Nantucket bakery and bought Portuguese bread her Mother smelled it and smiled and said, 'Pretty.'

Molly tried to make her understand where they were but nothing changed her Mother's mantra. Molly tried to see the dunes that she loved by herself. Seagulls flew over her head. Light oat grasses held on for dear life against the tides and winds. She picked green seaweed up and smelled its briny elements. Small shells clung to the seaweed and she picked them out neatly for her pockets.

When her Mother just plopped into the sand and did not want to walk any longer Molly feared that this was the end. Her Mother would be leaving her soon. How that could be she didn't know. It had all gone too fast. What could she say that she hadn't already said? Their intimacy was wordless now.

It was the kind of autumn that made her heart ache it was filled with so much beauty. Nantucket was asking her to look once more. It was the kind of visit when it was not possible to notice anyone else on the beach there in Mother/daughter intimacy.

Now her Mother dead.

The Christmas Stroll was in three days. Molly was ready to go now. She was moving herself away from solitude, she could not bear it again this December. She was completely healed from her accident in March and felt stronger after all the physical therapy. She wanted dancing nights. Couldn't she see a man she could turn to and smile at and maybe have him turn to her and smile back? It was worth the effort to find and pack her favorite bar dress she'd kept for years. She was going to take a bus to Hyannis and then take the ferry to Nantucket.

On the ferry ride she fell asleep. In her dreams, Molly saw John once again healthy and loving and smiling at her.

I can't believe you never lived there, John speaks from a dream.

She wakes when a youngster bumps into her legs as he runs about inside the ferry.

I can't believe you never lived there, John speaks to her again.

Weezie:
Nickname for Mary Louise

Dave the Chautauqua security guard found Maggie in her living room. She was sitting in her Mother's rocking chair reading. Dave had gone in to talk with her about the yearly art show coming to Bestor Plaza. Maggie was the chairperson organizing it. She always entered one of her Mother's small paintings of the Bell Tower in each show. Maggie was reading last week's *Chautauqua Daily* when Dave knocked and knocked on the unlocked front porch screen door.

Weezie didn't think she could make it through the funeral of her beloved childhood friend. They had been through everything together. They had just lived through the pandemic together. They braced each other up emotionally every day during the pandemic while working and playing cribbage until Maggie's small cribbage board began to lose its sheen. Weezie could tell Maggie anything. But she hadn't.

Weezie had relationships with guys but none turned into marriage. When Weezie was twenty-three she fell for a guy who worked with the Steamship Authority steering ferries back and forth from Nantucket and Martha's Vineyard to the Cape. She waitressed at the Chatham House that summer. She loved walking on the dunes with him when he had a break Cape-side. He told her all about the tanker that had split in two near the Chatham lighthouse. This well-read man with piercing blue eyes left for distant shores by joining the Merchant Marines the next summer. Weezie felt shipwrecked. But since they had not promised each other any enduring love how could she expect even a postcard?

Weezie found him living in Hyannis as a widower during the pandemic. They talked on the phone during their isolation as if nothing had ever washed in on the tide of a twenty-five-year absence. They were going to be in each other's lives once the pandemic ended and he had his back surgery. He had cracked vertebraes that needed mending. Weezie begged him not to go in for the surgery so soon. He went in anyway. The following week while learning to step on the parallel bars he collapsed with a heart attack and was gone.

Today is the day of Maggie's funeral and Weezie may just faint. She cannot go to the Presbyterian church in Westfield and say anything about Maggie. It would be too hard. Weezie knows the casket will be closed because Maggie always told her what she wanted at her service. It was always a kind of rainy-day joke between them that they would plan their funerals with the passages from poetry and the Bible and the music they each wanted played. Maggie wanted "*Ave Maria*" played from Andrea Boccelli's CD. Weezie planned to do this but she also went out and found the best tenor in the area to sing it live. *Ave Maria* twice was not too much for her dear friend. Weezie was hosting the after-funeral wake at her café. She shared five years of baking and catering with Maggie in their café. What had happened?

Maggie had a massive heart attack alone! Her heart

gave out and she was gone. Weezie was thankful Maggie never had to stay in a hospital. Maggie never wanted to be in the hospital with some disease.

Weezie walks into Maggie's home one last time. It is dark and the shadows bring an eerie feeling to all the furniture. Maggie had lots of photos of her Mother all around the living room. The kitchen was newly painted and Maggie had finally bought a stacked washer and dryer for the back shed. She had sent the strange clothes line of whirling arms made out of pipe to the Salvation Army. Though it had been her Mother's favorite for years.

In the night the house looks worn out and there is a stale smell to it. Weezie hates to smell the staleness creeping in so quickly. Maggie was always such a good housekeeper. She used Meyer's lemon and Murphy's soap and flowers to bring the outdoors inside. Maggie's house has been Weezie's home her whole life and there is nowhere else to be tonight as she sits in the rocker and cries.

The church parking lot is packed because Maggie was on so many committees. She was a member of the Chautauqua Garden Club and volunteered at the library. All the men and women she knew were attending the funeral. Weezie puts her arm through Dave's arm and they walk into the church. The scent of lilies is fragrant and intoxicating and reminds Weezie of Easter.

The day after the funeral Weezie begins to rethink her life. She didn't go to Fredonia and get a master's in the culinary arts. And she wonders why. She remembers looking at real estate there because sometimes she got sick of living in a small apartment over the café. She finds a dentist and has her back molar checked. She thought it had to be extracted but he told her, *No it did not.* She was happy with that news. Suddenly she is having backaches and her bowels are backing up on her. With all the pasta and beer and fries she has consumed for five years it is no wonder. Every night she puts her electric tens on her stomach to calm down the blockage.

Weezie lives a sad quiet grief for five months but today she feels like a prisoner. She has heard the Canadian geese flying overhead to the south. The trees have lost their autumnal beauty. She has weaved the moments together with Maggie from childhood and adulthood over and over in memory until she has threads dripping through her heart that will remain forever. Maggie is gone. Her life is cut from Weezie. The words ring like a bell. The Bell Tower sounds its noon chimes Ding! Ding! Ding! Ding! Ding! Ding!

Ding! Ding! Ding! Ding! Ding! Ding!

This is a fact this is the truth. The bells ring all over the lake up to Lake Erie across New York state into New England.

The gates around Chautauqua Institution hem her in. She has become its prisoner. Her body and mind talk to her and tell her *she cannot stay.*

Up in the attic over the café where she kept her mementos sit ferry tickets from her one and only trip to Nantucket when she was young. It was during her college years at the University of Pittsburgh.

She climbs the steep stairs to the attic. She sits down on the old wooden floor and opens the trunk. Weezie remembers how she and Maggie loved the movie ***Little Women*** with Susan Sarandon and Wynona Ryder. Maggie and Weezie both cried at the scene when Jo opens Beth's trunk and discovers all her cherished mementos.

Now Weezie cries in her own moment of cherished memories.

Andrea: Quaker Woman

Andrea stands quietly while gravediggers lower her Mother into the ground. Clumps of earth cover the simple coffin. She stands apart from the large gathering of members in silent homage. It is late November and the chill makes her shiver. Out in the bay there are white caps.

It is a Quaker burial. No prayers are offered as it is not the way. Only a few quiet words are spoken in gratitude for the deceased. Her Mother a devout Quaker was a kind woman. Everyone is dressed in gray and black like the darkening clouds swirling in the sky the week before Thanksgiving. The little burial ground is showing signs of disuse. Hummocks of grass and sand cover the newer graves. There are no headstones. Andrea is glad her Mother requested being buried in the Old Ground near other Quakers from the last three hundred years.

Faces are quiet and set in a mixture of grief and acceptance. It is not their way to wail and sheen or to have a big party and wake like the Irish. Quaker burials, like their meetings for worship, are essentially quiet affairs, devoid of ceremony. Andrea thinks her Mother is now at peace. For Friends, death is the end of the life thee knows and what comes after remains a mystery. It is enough that a life has brought joy and love. Andrea knows her Mother is somewhere in an eternal place.

Andrea is not joining anyone after the burial. She often thinks she will leave the faith altogether but something always brings her back to the Spirit of Truth she once experienced as a child with her Mother at Quaker meetings.

The walk back home filled with memories of her Mother is a silent one. She has the chance to be quiet without the others. She pictures her Mother and knows she must guard what she sees in her mind's eye before time and the world rob her of her memories.

In the Quaker Meetings Andrea had to be careful

not to let her dismay show for any of the new ways the Meetings were going. They were hanging on by a thread and if she showed any irregularity in her conduct, particularly in relation to marriage, it was grounds for being turned out. Forgiveness, while present, became a passive rather than an active principle in the years of dwindling membership.

It was more important than ever to be sure of the fidelity of the membership to Quaker principles. In the past, irregularities in behavior had been addressed in a communal spirit: confrontation, apology, and forgiveness. But this way was changing rapidly. Andrea remembers as a child the grave looks from the Ministers whenever she and her cousins giggled in the youth gallery. They finally asked schoolmasters to sit with the children for Meetings to keep them quiet.

Now she was a woman of forty-nine and she could hardly depend on a schoolmaster to curtail her need to oppose a rule or to keep her from letting out a laugh at some ridiculous remark.

When Andrea, a true beauty, looked around the Meeting House she could not see any future husband.

So many of the men were married. She hadn't married at the usual age of twenty-five or twenty-eight and she was not breeding children every year.

She was respected in town because she and her Mother ran the weaving and yarn shop called Yarn Pastures. A lovelier place on the island was hard to find. The sheep were local so the yarns dyed from berries and plants on the island were the best in New England. Her internet business had flourished and she was a self-supporting woman. Many people married out of Meeting but she knew that would rip her Mother's memory to threads. Much energy was now spent in Meeting determining which apologies were sincere, if someone married outside, and which were merely expedient.

In the past, the fifteen-year-old Quakers, considered full adult members, bothered the older generation. It seemed there was a breakdown in the social order and they were beginning to mingle socially with outsiders. They were keeping company with the Congregationalists and one couple had married as first cousins so they were disowned. The Congregationalist men sought out Quaker women because they knew they were good with handling money. Many Quakers had left the island entirely and gone to other Meeting Houses in Nova Scotia and New Bedford and some to the Carolinas.

Andrea knew about a Quaker man who at age forty-two had tried to marry a woman who was found guilty only through rumors of homosexual activity. He and his intended wife were shunned by the Nantucket Meeting's security measures. He left to return to Newfoundland. The woman of rumor left the island for Nova Scotia. Another case that bothered Andrea's sense of right and wrong was the man accused of fathering an illegitimate child with a non-Quaker waitress. The woman was shunned and sent away. The man later married a Quaker woman who raised the child with no repercussions toward either of them.

Andrea knew of all these horror stories from the past three hundred years but she never experienced anything cruel or unfair. It was why she felt split with the whole religion. It was why she could feel fear within herself at the idea of something terribly wrong happening to her inside a Meeting. The way she lived was exemplary but it left her doubting her own mind some days.

She did not like the feeling of one moment not leading to the next now that her Mother was dead. Before life flowed and she did not look at her fellow Quakers as if she were a doe-in-headlights. She had to stay silent in Meetings so she would not cry with her own confusion. She tried to tell herself she had no face to look at and no man was looking. And no minister was looking at her. Andrea had never spoken in a Meeting. She loved the silence and the centering that took place. She respected anyone who did speak with the Spirit.

Now she was unsure why she was cvcn contemplating someone at this age. She knew she had to be right about any choice if she was to remain a Quaker. Perhaps it was the loss of her Mother and the feeling of being really alone for the first time. Andrea had lost her father to lung cancer ten years before. She was an only child. She had good Quaker women friends as that was a built-in part of the culture of Nantucket. Women had been there for three centuries running the island and its finances while the men went off whaling all over the world for several years.

But it was the Sunday after Thanksgiving that she

sat in Meeting when a young girl named Mary was sobbing in front of the women. Mary was twenty and she and her boyfriend who worked on the docks unloading the trucks of food had found themselves in love and making love.

The Minister spoke:

Thee knows that the Lord forgives all transgressions of those who come seeking the Truth.

Thee must make apology Mary and it must come from thy heart. Thee and the Lord will know if what thee feels and what thee speaks come from the Truth.

Andrea begins to squirm with the shame she sees in Mary.

Mary speaks again. Is thee the first to be in this way?

No, the Minister answers. There are many in the community who have fallen to temptation. Thee is a good girl and thee helps thee's Mother with the business while thee's father works offshore. Thee must think deeply on this and make thee's apology not only to all gathered but to God who thou must satisfy with words and prayers.

Mary spoke: It was love at first sight. Thee walked the dunes and looked at maps to see where Nantucket stood on the globe. Thee is born of Portuguese parents and grandparents on Nantucket. How can thee understand the waters far away if elders send thee away? The island and each other are thee's love. Andre will take care of thee and as thee knows thee is a good bookkeeper. Thee have mercy.

The elders and Ministers consulted each other in a huddle.

Andrea held her breath. She wanted an affirmative answer so she could hold onto the Quaker faith longer – she told herself if they ostracized and banished this sweet young woman Andrea would leave the Quaker Meeting House forever.

The room was silent.

Finally, the Minister turned to Mary.

We the elders and Ministers have heard thy truth and we do accept thee's apology. We will allow the marriage and the union of thee and Andre and the birth of a child will banish all mention of this ever again.

Andrea thought: *they are still trying to show a worthy face to the world after all the schisms.*

Andrea walked with Mary outside and asked her to come to the yarn shop.

They did not talk. When they went inside Yarn Pastures Andrea showed Mary all the beautiful baby clothes and blankets.

Pick one Mary.

Oh thee is too good.

No, thee is good. Please pick a blanket the women have all donated blankets.

For all newborns.

Mary eyed the colors of heather and witches-broom and sand woven into tiny little blankets.

This one.

Andrea wrapped it up and gave Mary the bag.

Thank thee.

Thee was very brave today, Mary.

Mary turned and left the store.

Andrea watched her walk down Main Street.

STRAINING HER EYES TOWARD Brant Point Weezie knew she was coming into harbor. She walked along not as sure of herself today as she had been in her youth.

She walked into the Visitor's Center and asked for a room. The welcome lady behind the counter asked her how long she wanted to stay.

Weezie thought for a moment.

A month maybe more.

The woman texted a property and got an answer right back.

Le Languedoc has an opening but then I'm afraid you would have to leave if you stay longer. They shut down after the stroll....it's not far...up two streets. It's a queen bed and private bath, will that suit you?

Great.

Are there taxis here anymore?

A few but if you don't have much you can walk very easily.

I think I need a taxi.

I'll call for one.

The woman texted again.

He's outside now, Island Cab.

Weezie went outside, arranged her two bags and backpack and got in.

Hi.

Hi.

24 Broad.

Sure.

The driver pulled up to Le Languedoc.

I'll help you with your bags.

Thanks. Weezie gave him a tip.

He took them to the second floor of the inn.

Weezie followed behind him.

Once she closed the door she collapsed in the wing chair.

MOLLY COULD SEE THE UNITARIAN DOME. The ferry pulled into Steamboat Wharf. She grabbed her bags and made her way to the Periwinkle Inn.

She unpacked quickly. Then she walked to the Brotherhood. It was jam-packed and hard to find a table alone so they put her at the end of a larger table. She didn't mind she felt the excitement of the stroll immediately. She ordered a veggieburger, fries and three Pina Coladas to get in the mood.

The Dreamland Theatre was her first stop after her meal. She looked at the movie marquee. They were playing *It's A Wonderful Life* all weekend and giving a silver bell to the first 100 people. What a dream to see it on the large screen again.

She stopped in the Visitor's Center and picked up a schedule. She wanted to go on the historic stroll tomorrow afternoon and knew she could find Federal and India. She wanted to go buy a few soy candles at the Stop 'N Shop parking lot and then she saw a new item listed: a staged adaptation of one of Elin's books. Oh, she couldn't miss that. She was a real fan of Hilderbrand's books.

A radio program on WCAI at the Visitor's Center blares news and music for tomorrow's Christmas Stroll. Molly hears Yarn Pastures announced as a lovely place to shop for all your knitting friends. She walks back to her room at the Periwinkle.

Outside on the sidewalk Santa Claus holds children on his lap while they have their picture taken. The day sparkles with a soft sunlight and temperatures are in the high 40s with no wind. It is perfect. All the Canadian geese dip their beaks into Hummock Pond. The winter birds flutter in their new location.

Standing here now in thee's kitchen with cup of coffee and keys time to go to the shop and begin to smile and sell to the happy visitors Andrea hears her shop Yarn Pastures announced on WCAI Stop at Hub and buy a newspaper first then stand in town and watch the strangers for a moment No thread of connection at all Watch the horses parade around with Santa Watch the drivers in the cars grow impatient Wish there were no cars allowed on Main today if only the town council would pass that rule Watch the tour buses unload Lost in thoughts dreading that the infrastructure of water, sewers and electricity will collapse during this invasion

Standing here in the room at the Periwinkle memories flow through Molly when she was younger and visited Nantucket When she brought her husband when she brought her Mother Where are my keys Never remember where anything small is anymore Keys and cell phone and lipstick and blush and pen Panic over and over and living alone only exacerbates it Wasting time looking and looking

Standing here in the breakfast room Looking at the table with its fresh coffee and fruit and muffins Scene so beautiful Weezie hears Yarn Pastures announced on WCAI holding my keys buttoning my winter coat Pulling on my hat and gloves Ready to go off to the whole damn world of Nantucket this morning and enjoy the stroll What surprises might happen

A NEW CUSTOMER WALKED IN. Weezie didn't knit but she loved to touch the yarn. It was such a lovely sensation. She wanted so much to create something but the thought of needles and that kind of patience was not something she possessed.

Andrea left her to browse through the selections.

If thee needs any help.

Weezie's head turned upward from the yarn.

Thee? she thought. My god a Quaker, really? How do I say anything back?

Weezie did not know how to address this lovely woman. She saw nothing but the sunlight streaming in and down on all the colorful yarns.

Maggie would strike up a conversation. Maggie would know all about the Friends on Nantucket by the time she had finished browsing.

Weezie wanted to buy a gift. She thought of her half-sister in Arizona. Katherine was divorced but she had a little boy who was four. Weezie looked at the little sweaters.

It was hot in Arizona but there were cool nights. She bought a rust-colored sweater.

Weezie took it to the counter where Andrea stood.

Oh, that is lovely.

Weezie got her credit card out and tapped it on the machine.

While she stood there she looked at the tiny woven coin purses.

Andrea finished the transaction and wrapped the sweater.

What happened to your hand? Weezie asked.

Andrea had wrapped an ace bandage around her wrist that morning.

Oh arthritis some mornings. Not too serious. Is thee visiting the Christmas Stroll?

Yes, here for my first stroll, never been, over at the Languedoc.

She pauses.

I don't mean to be rude but are you a Quaker?

Yes. Thee are a small group now.

I didn't mean to pry.

Thee didn't.

Thanks again.

Weezie left the store.

She wondered how her little nephew would like the sweater.

Weezie spent last Christmas with Katherine in Phoenix drinking Margaritas and horseback riding in the hills around her sister's home. Weezie nearly fell off the horse but Katherine was a good horse-woman. Just not a good wife. She loved her work as a lawyer but she loved to boss everyone around so they eventually left. They often felt she was inter-rogating them on the witness stand. Katherine had a hard time separating her work from her marriage. She wasn't the best mother either but she did get nannies in to keep her son fed and bathed.

The next few hours Weezie walked Main Street. She picked out violets at the farmers' market. All the stores were decorated. Candles were already in the windows. It felt like living inside a Christmas card at night. Weezie thought. She was glad she was here. No summer swims or chasing the waves today. She was in town and shopping called to her. She looked inside many of the shops for starfish ornaments and lavender bath salts. She found both. She thought it would be best to not overshop. She wanted to come back and stroll the next day too and be so excited by the day she would buy herself something wonderful. Too bad she could not buy Maggie a gift. Maggie would love it here on Nantucket.

Weezie called her friend Biggs back at the lake.

You're there then?

I'm here.

Any snow?

None.

We got hit again Buffalo got 10 inches and we got 6.

Glad I'm missing it.

Okay. When ya coming back?

A month maybe longer.

Let me know if you need anything.

Don't worry.

Love ya.

Me you.

Weezie hung up. She was better here than at the lake. She knew that much. She felt desire again. Books and stroll ornaments and people. Oh the strangers marching along to the Christmas tunes. Look at the magic of this place. She went to the Hub to buy the latest *Inquirer and Mirror*. Then she walked to the Downy Flake and ordered coffee and donuts.

She spread her delights across the table. She placed a napkin in her lap. She was beginning to relax.

Nantucket could do that.

The island fifteen miles long and three across could spit out stress into its dunes and waves in a short time. The islanders knew this secret. But not many summer people came in the winter months and the most beautiful month of the year, October, was often left to nature and the cranberry bogs which were now shrinking because of competition from Canada. The biologists were going to let them return to their original source: wet lands and wild flowers and peat. Once again the lesson of impermanence.

Weezie suddenly thought of her body. What could she do after this donut splurge? How could she move her body in the month of December?

If she could paint she might join a class indoors. Do they still do plein-air in December, probably not but there was no snow on the ground so maybe some brave souls set up their French easels. But she hadn't painted for years and then only in acrylic.

Perhaps a yoga class. She looked in the classified ads for a yoga class. Yes there was one at 7 a.m. at Dionis Beach the next day. She would make herself get to it.

Her next impulse took her to Murry's where she bought a pair of Nantucket Reds, a shirt and a pair of Sperry Topsiders. Now she felt better. Her walk was freer and surer. In the dressing room she saw that the skin of her cheeks looked brighter. Her eyes looked less like dead fish eyes. Her dishwater hair hung medium length with a small bang sticking out under her new Nantucket cap.

She was just an off-islander. Who did she know? No one. She had once planned a reunion with a college friend but that fell through. Weezie was here to mourn the death of her best friend, Maggie. Yet something was stirring. She carried her bags outside and glanced at herself in the window pane. Not as young she thought. She didn't care the clothes made her happy and she hadn't felt a happy moment in six months.

She drifted along and found herself at the Whaling Museum at the foot of Steamboat Wharf. She paid the admission and began to walk underneath the skeleton of a jawbone from a huge sperm whale hanging from the ceiling. She found the whaleboat that sailed 3500 miles in ninety-three days with the crew of the *Essex*. She had watched the Ron Howard movie.

Weezie kept wandering through other rooms where she saw portraits of whaling captains, sea chests, medicine chests, relics from the Pacific Islands and logbooks. She loved reading the logbooks.

When she left the museum she looked up and saw the gold dome of a church. She headed toward it. She found out it was the Unitarian church. A bell rang at noon. The clock tower was used before the days of fire alarms as a watchtower for fires. The watchman would signal by waving a lantern in the general direction of any blaze that had been sighted. The $500 dollar bell was cast in Portugal and brought to Nantucket by a sea captain in the 18th century.

With no map she kept wandering through little lanes and streets. She had read that nowhere in America could one wander among so many lanes and streets composed of dwellings that were built in the 18th and 19th century. The Widows Walk she had heard of really did exist, the grey shingled houses, the beautiful doorways and white fences of another time. There were still flowers and holly blooming in doorways in December!

The light of Nantucket was flooding her heart. She

didn't know there was light or feeling left in her. She wanted to say Maggie was alive, that the truth of a few months ago when Maggie talked with her every day was still surrounding her in her world but she had been gutted. She could barely climb up the stairs after a day at the café. After the funeral she decided she would be solitary. No one would know her. Why talk and eat and make up other activities with others now? Maggie was gone. Her best friend in her whole life was gone.

Come to me pain. Throw your crushing tentacles around me. Keep me from breathing. Try it and I will let you in for a moment then tear you out. I am here on Nantucket. I have given myself this much. Tears will dry.

She walked to the post office and mailed the package to Arizona. The solitude around her was the island. If she could feel its shores and earth under her feet the swells of sadness would leave her, she thought.

Weezie entered the library and looked up the history of Quakers on Nantucket.

She sat down and read.

Great Mary's Children June 28, 1702

A visiting minister has come to Nantucket, Mary Coffin Starbuck has issued an open invitation to a Meeting for Worship that she will hold in her home, known as Parliament House. The preacher is a Quaker.....

She read on about the weeping of Mary Coffin Starbuck from the preacher's inspiring words about not feeling anger, hatred, greed, and envy. The world would be a much better place, the preacher tells everyone…

Weezie stopped after a half hour.

She wandered around and noticed the children's library with the name Weezie.

How ironic. Weezie thought.

She asked the librarian why it was named Weezie.

A little girl of ten was riding her horse and she fell off and died. Her parents started this library with funding and named it the Weezie children's library, she answered.

Was it long ago?

1959.

Oh I wonder if her name was Mary Louise like mine?

I don't know.

What a sad thing.

Yes, it's a lovely library.

I see that. Do you have *Winnie the Pooh?*

Oh yes back in the stacks over there.

Thanks.

Weezie browsed through the books and picked out her favorite: ***Winnie the Pooh.***

Why not?

MOLLY HEADED FOR THE STOP 'N SHOP parking lot to buy candles. She walked down Main and over to the parking lot. She was just picking up green soy candles when she heard her name called.

Molly is that you?

Molly turned around and saw Weezie. They hugged.

You haven't changed at all and it's what three years?

I can't believe this. What brings you here?

I just had to get away. It's my Christmas gift to me.

I know I know….are you here with anyone?

Solo.

Me too.

Let's do the Club Car for lunch before it fills up.

Sure, isn't it close by?

Right over there.

I love these candles. Molly pays for her six green candles.

She puts her arm through Weezie's and they stroll over to the Club Car.

They take a seat by the window. The piano player is belting out Christmas tunes already.

A waiter brings the menus.

Would you like something to drink?

Oh, yes do you have any spiked eggnog?

I'll have the same.

Tell me how are you?

It's hard. You know she was my best friend from childhood and she died of a massive heart attack… alone.

Molly listens with compassion.

I hate she was all alone. Now I'm just missing everything! The café, which I sold, the people and cooking. I really loved cooking with Maggie.

So sad.

The waiter brings their drinks right on time.

Let's toast Maggie, Molly suggests.

They clink glasses.

To Maggie.

And to us finding each other here. What a coincidence.

The piano player sings "Let It Snow."

This is my first stroll….I can't remember did you come before?

No my first too.

Their chowder and sourdough bread arrive and they dig in.

They both turn quiet.

Molly remembers the last few reunions with Weezie when they met in Santa Fe. They both missed the reunion in Savannah. So they have not seen each other for three years. Molly loved the Santa Fe reunion. Staying at the La Fonda and eating in every well-known restaurant in town especially the Pink Adobe. She broke her vow to not eat meat that night and ordered the famous steak served medium rare.

Weezie takes another piece of sourdough bread.

God this is good. I know John is gone. What's it been two, three?

Four years already.

I brought him here for a few weeks before he died. We stayed out in S'conset with some friends of mine. I love S'conset.

I know you do…I think it's great you are giving yourself this time here.

I'm living as best as I can. But I do keep getting thoughts of the end they just won't stop. It was horrible. The cancer peeled away everything I knew John to be. He got thinner and thinner and bones stuck out everywhere. And his labored breathing just killed me or I wish it had.

They are both silent.

I've been a nurse and seen a lot and this was bad. I felt helpless.

I'm so sorry Molly. Try to see good things while you are here now.

Yes, let's move on. I am here to enjoy the island I love.

They pay and leave the Club Car. It is getting darker outside.

I think I am going back to my room for a nap I'm feeling tired.

Maybe all those eggnogs we had.

Want to join me at the Dreamland tonight? They're putting on an adaptation of one of Elin's winter books.

Sure.

What time?

Meet me at 6:45 p.m. It starts at 7 p.m.

They hug.

So glad you're here Weezie.

Same here. See you tonight.

CHARLES RIVERS DROVE AROUND THE ROADS of S'conset and looked out at the ocean as it opened to the moonlight. There were the huge mansions that he helped to renovate or build. What was he thinking? These hedge-fund managers, politicians, businessmen, lawyers, and doctors. His first venture into real estate had been a complete success; he renovated the abandoned tavern in Charlestown, Massachusetts. He formed a new company called the Charlestown Development Company and went on to renovate several historic buildings that lay dormant waiting for the right person to bring them back to life.

On Nantucket it was a different story. The small cottages owned by African Americans in S'conset were either falling into the sea from hurricanes or were being sold to new investors. He stepped in at the right time and began managing projects for this new breed of visitor with millions of dollars to spend.

As he rode along happy to see the Summer House

and the Chanticleer still standing and operating as restaurants he is horrified by his own greed. These mansions now go from two to twenty million and some eat up the land with the buildings. These millionaires never want anyone to go to the beach on their tract of land. The S'conset beach has been open for 250 years to anyone who wanted to walk to the dunes.

O his ulterior motive sometimes verged on the grotesque. He was in business with these millionaires and the men were in New York or London while the attractive affluent wives were left on-island talking to Charles. He often lusted after them and once or twice did find himself in the guest bedroom naked and hot. It was all very discreet. It ruined his marriage. He was willing to let that go. He was happy as a 'pig in shit' and he knew it.

Now driving around in December in the fifth decade of the Christmas Stroll, Charles was happy so many people visited with their wallets bulging with credit cards. It all gave him a warm feeling in his Midas heart. But then without any warning his chest began to tighten and his right eye did not focus on the headlights or the sea or road by the Summer House.

He knew there was a steep embankment across the street with wooden steps to the beach. It was often a place to take a woman after cocktails at the bar. Walk her down the steps and to the beach and then of course back up the steep steps. Now spinning around the road with pain in his left arm and his right eye totally blind. He is having trouble breathing. He pulls the car over and stops. He breathes in and out in and out hard…*breathe deep and thank the ocean* was his favorite magnet on his refrigerator.

No, not now. Not in this sad look back at his life of greed here. What had he done for anyone else all this time here on Nantucket? Nothing only watched the mansions go up and the real estate prices in the *Inq and Mirror* get more and more expensive. When he came here the last price he remembered was $350,000 for a cottage and it was sold to some woman who wanted street lights installed immediately around the paths that led down from her cottage to the beach in S'conset. Street lights! What was she afraid of the boogeyman?

Where did the dollar go? It surpassed anything even he could understand. Greed here in this pain. He should get out and slide down the embankment and just call it a day. One more stupid choice. One more alone moment.

Here he was about ready to slide or thinking about it but he wasn't actually out of the car yet. What is that? Headlights? They are stopping. An officer sticks a flashlight into his face.

You alright? Why it's Charles Rivers. Hey bring an ambulance out here, he calls in. In front of the Summer House…S'conset.

Can you walk?

No, my legs are cramped.

THE COTTAGE HOSPITAL WAS NEW. If one had to go to a hospital it was not the worst place to be. They brought Charles Rivers into the emergency room where nurses and EMTs huddled around him. Blood pressure, IVs. The usual routine for a stroke or TIA. They admitted him immediately. He slept the rest of the night.

In the morning he looked out the window at the scrub oak.

Something could sooth him now. If only there was a person in the whole world who could say hello. No wife no children. Only his money and what good was it now?

His tongue was dry. His view out the window: now seagulls. To see a face that held promise. Could his face look at someone's face now that he was still alive? An unshaven sixty-year-old. He recoiled from himself. His time was served and now how many years or even days did he have left? Did his mansions come see him last night? What did save him?

MOLLY WALKED INTO THE VOLUNTEER'S OFFICE at the hospital and asked if she could help for a few hours. She wanted to bring Christmas Stroll cheer to anyone who was there. Her nursing background was the reason the volunteer coordinator agreed to Molly helping.

Here are the flowers we are giving out today.

Molly rolled a cart filled with flowers to the second floor. She stopped in the first room.

Hello. You are Mrs. Gannon. The little woman in bed looked about 85.

I have some flowers for you today. Molly went to the bed and helped her sit up. I'll put them in this vase right here.

Mrs. Gannon smiled. Oh thank you dear. You're so kind. Is it Christmas?

No not yet but we are celebrating the Christmas Stroll.

Oh, I remember.

Molly rolled the cart to the next room. Charles Rivers was sitting up in bed.

Molly stopped the cart.

Charles?

Charles was groggy.

Molly went to the side of his bed.

Charles Rivers from Charlestown and the tavern?

Charles smiled.

It's Molly. Remember the book club meetings? What are you doing here? I mean here in the hospital. I heard you came to the island.

Charles points to the glass of water.

Molly lifts it to his lips.

I live here.

How are you feeling? Was it a heart attack?

Just about nearly TAI…I mean TIA...stroke. I guess. They say I can go home later today.

Good. Is someone picking you up and taking you home?

No. Not really. Just my driver.

Let me.

Charles looks into her eyes.

Molly leaves the flowers.

He watches her leave as if he has just had a dream. Doped up on pills. Why would she pick him up later?

He hardly knows her.

MOLLY KNELT IN St Mary's Catholic Church. She prayed for Charles and lit a candle. Molly hadn't practiced her faith for years but something about seeing Charles moved her to walk to church.

What could it mean that they collided like two planets? Fate was not a word she used. It always felt like whatever she had in her life came from work and fortitude. There were no coincidences she could see. She didn't really know what synchronistic meant. Molly never took the Jungian courses for her nursing training.

It did give her pause though to see Charles. The moment felt immense in her heart. Maybe she could stay longer. Molly had nothing to rush back to just an elf fund and the VA auction of trees.

How many hours could she calculate in wasted time? She had done nothing really since John died. She was very expert at sitting in front of the TV at night watching Netflix. Her peers always told her what they were excited about watching. They'd ask: *have you seen? Lessons in Chemistry* was hot now. But where were her own lessons? What were they? She gave her life to nursing others and John and her Mother. Now she had nothing left. Zero vitality. This is what she packed for Nantucket. Zero vitality.

Molly looked at the statue of the Virgin Mary. She did not say a *Hail Mary*. She had no formal prayer inside her. But she thought she heard a whisper from somewhere in her mind. Could it be her hopes for a new lover whispering to her? Was Charles resting now? Was he the prayer Molly could hear?

Molly stood up, genuflected, made the sign of the Cross and left the church.

MOLLY ARRIVES AT THE DOORS OF THE COTTAGE HOSPITAL. Charles Rivers is being pushed in a wheelchair by an aide. The front door opens. Charles smooths his hair. He is dissatisfied with his appearance. Molly moves instinctively. She takes the handles of the wheelchair and pushes. Ronny, his all-around assistant, arrives to drive his boss home in the BMW.

Hey, I'm Ronny.

I'm Molly.

She and Ronny help Charles into the back seat. She gets in the front passenger seat. Strangers keep going in and out of the hospital door. Molly is a stranger in the car.

Charles closes his eyes for a moment, then opens them.

My home's in Monomoy. Outskirts of town.

Ronny drives slowly from the hospital. When he pulls into the circular driveway in Monomoy Molly silences a swoon.

The grounds and house are gorgeous. The large shingled, gray classic Nantucket home spreads across lawns and gardens. The home is not one of the new mansions Charles built. Molly observes a few gardeners bringing in summer patio furniture in December.

Ronny stops the car and helps Charles out of the back seat. Charles uses his will of steel to walk but his legs are too weak. The gardeners come running across the lawn to help him.

Mr. Rivers, Mr. Rivers, welcome home sir.

No, no, wheelchair.

They put their arms around his waist and help him walk to the door.

Molly follows behind. She enters the front door. Everything stands still as she glances at the ornate front hall and big rooms off to the left and right.

Oh how different you and I. Can we find anything that can bridge this difference? Can we give something to each other? Would it be need? Could it be fondness? Could it be companionship? Could it grow into love?

Charles calls to her. The gardeners have taken Charles to the large study.

Molly.

She steps through the rooms and finds her way to the study. She sees a cot set up for him.

I'll sleep here so I can get to the kitchen.

He smiles his first smile.

Yes, good idea.

He sits in a big chair. Molly grabs a Nantucket blanket off the cot and places it over his shoulders. She leaves her arm next to his for a moment. He slides his hand up her arm. Molly closes her eyes and takes a deep sigh.

Are you alright?

Yes.

Would you like a drink?

Oh, no, much too early for me.

I think I'll have one.

Ronny.

Ronny returns.

Ronny, get me a Scotch out there.

Yes, sir. Ronny goes to the bar area and pours a Scotch. He brings it back to Charles and hands it to him.

Cheers, lifting his glass to Molly.

I best be going.

Must you?

You need your rest now. In fact rest all day. But I can stop by later if you'd like.

I'd like. Will ten be too late?

No not at all. I'll be finished at the stroll by then.
Perfect.

Ronny will give you a ride back to town.

Yes, thank you, Charles.

See you tonight, Molly…

They lock eyes.

Molly walks to the front door. Her heart pounding.

FANTASIES BEGAN once Ronny was down the driveway with Molly.

Charles let out a belch. And poured himself another Scotch. Oh, it wouldn't take long to plunge himself into her. He could see his hands holding those strong hips. She looks fine. Probably a little younger than I am. She's a beautiful woman. Not wanting to wait long to seduce her. Can he do it? He was letting himself get hot in his groin. His brain had the TIA not his testicles. Molly what a lovely name so Irish sounding but was she? Didn't sound like Irish lilt when she spoke. She seemed strong to him and fluttery too like a beautiful Monarch across his tired eyes. Molly! He liked her name.… well she'll be back and we can do our dance of flirting like women love to do…he'll have to take a shower with Ronny's help and put on some Old Spice…so traditional. He wanted his body to touch hers. He wanted her. Could he even think of love again?

He lit a cigarette and inhaled. Not my time to die am

sure of it...going into town next week for a business meeting at the Bistro at Le Languedoc. See my buddies from Charlestown. What a wonder to say hello to Molly at the tavern years back and here she is helping me home from the hospital on Nantucket. What luck or was it? What was it, chance? Serendipity? Not my karma …it's too evil. What can it mean?

He inhaled again. He was quieter now. Love with Molly. Could he move himself out of his own selfishness? He had been divorced for ten years. This could be sweet again, very sweet. He willed himself to see an affair with Molly… seducing Molly for the first time and hoped his mechanics down there would warm up and work for him since he never believed in Viagra. An old man if he couldn't rise to the challenge of a woman once more.

MOLLY SAT IN THE CAR with Ronny in silence. She felt the softness of the seat. She held her scarf around her neck. Now dusk was approaching outside in the December light. She hurried to her room after saying thank you to Ronny.

She thought to herself must get to the theatre. But first a bath to calm her nerves. Should she tell Weezie about this afternoon and Charles? The bath water flows 'round her body and cools her burning mind.

Too much in my head…she splashes water over her face and body and hair.

Her hair must smell fragrant to him. He will touch it with his hands. Those strong hands have lifted a hammer or two and held an architect's pencil. She pictured running her hands through his strawberry blond wavy hair. His three-day old chin hair sent butterflies to her empty stomach. His square face and pale eyes sent shivers down her spine. Astounded that he could open up her heart so quickly she began to daydream while telling herself to chant AUMs to calm down.

WEEZIE CLIMBS OUT OF THE JEEP she rented at Young's Bicycle Shop. She sees Molly in front of the theatre. They greet each other again with hugs and walk into the Dreamland. After the show they walk outside into the night.

How does she come up with all those stories?

I have no idea. I wonder: what is my story?

I know what you mean. Well shall we go to the Brotherhood and see if it starts there? Weezie laughs.

Sure.

Want a ride over?

Oh…you got a Jeep.

Yep.

Wow. You know I'd like to walk a bit in the air. I'll meet you there.

Are you okay, Molly?

Fine. Meet you at the Brotherhood.

Weezie leaves in the Jeep. On impulse she drives down Main Street before heading for the Brotherhood. She stops in front of Yarn Pastures and parks.

Wedges of light reflect the yarns in colors of sky blue, heather, cranberry and witches-broom on all the tables and shelves. Weezie stands on the sidewalk looking in the window. She can see a small desk light still burning.

Andrea works out her calculations from the day's business.

Weezie wonders to herself: *why is she standing here in time and space as the procession of the stroll winds down?*

MOLLY FEELS THE DARKNESS cover the houses and the waters in Nantucket harbor. The people are going home now or to a bar. A day of the stroll is over.

She walks into the busy Brotherhood and takes a table in the corner. A popular band is playing Christmas tunes. A waiter comes over.

Just you?

No, I'm meeting a friend.

Weezie walks in.

Over here, Weezie.

Weezie has a smile on her face.

Molly wonders what has happened between the Dreamland Theatre and the Brotherhood.

The waiter stands waiting.

Two glasses of Veuve Clicquot no better yet…the whole bottle!

The whole bottle! Wow what are we celebrating?

Molly keeps looking at Weezie's glow.

You tell me.

What?

You found something?

Yeah, my studio for a month and the Jeep and tomorrow I go pick up a foster dog. How great is all that?

Where are you staying?

In Surfside. Out of Le Languedoc tomorrow. Am I really grinning?

Yes, you are girl. Weezie, what guts to just make a decision like that to stay and a puppy…… but I know ……I understand

I don't know…

Alright, alright, don't go all glum on me. We can

share that's what friends are for. Should we break into *You've Got A Friend*?

Weezie laughs.

They both love Carole King.

I'm glad you're here, Molly, no really. It's such a coincidence. Go ahead...what are you looking so radiant about? And that red blouse is dynamite. I couldn't see it in the theatre.

Thank you. I thought I'd put on my favorite tonight to be festive. So let me tell you about today…it's been a strange day.

How strange?

The waiter brings the bottle of Veuve Clicquot.

Thank you.

He pours the champagne into long-stemmed glasses that sparkle.

Molly waits for him to leave.

I helped Charles Rivers out of the Cottage Hospital

back to his home in Monomoy.

Charles Rivers? Who's he? You lost me!

You must remember the man from Charlestown where I used to live you remember?

Oh I think I know your book club right?

Yeah, that man. The one I used to say hello to in the tavern.

Wow he's here?

I went to the hospital and there he was.

You went to the hospital are you sick?

No I just wanted to feel my nurse me inside a beautiful hospital so I volunteered to take flowers around to patients and there he was.

You know you're…

The waiter returned.

I'm done with my shift so Todd will be your server.

Okay could you tell him to bring another?

Sure.

What?

Weezie wasn't sure what she was saying before.

This is our type of fun, huh, Weezie?

You bet, so many afternoons in college and at our reunions. So go on…

So there he was laid up in a hospital bed. He'd had a TIA. But they fixed him up and sent him home today.

Oh my god. This is like a dream huh? What happened?

I got him settled he drank a glass of Scotch and I left.

Where does he live?

A beautiful home in Monomoy.

Wow. Weezie's eyes were glazing over but she was

already following her old friend's fantasy of something happening with Charles and then Molly would live on the island.

We didn't hold hands. My own brain cannot look at a blank canvas it fills with the past so quickly….it's my problem…. but the past is gone isn't it, Weezie?

It truly is.

So what do I do with the mind wasting so many moments on this and that since John died what has any of it led up to is there someone to sit with at the end of the day how many more trips can I take even if my accountant tells me to take a trip every year oh okay take a trip so I go to Morocco and Spain and Costa Rica and who knows where? Still coming home to the same empty place! Sometimes I think thoughts are as tiring as the trips on buses with strangers.

Okay okay I hear this, god Molly, you are really going deep on me, huh? More champagne?

Molly nods.

Every book I read takes me off to a new adventure

and I want to go. But do I want to do this the rest of my life? I'm fifty-two.

Weezie pours another glass of champagne for both of them.

Thanks.

Molly, clean the cobwebs and get into this one gift to yourself here and now on Nantucket for the Christmas Stroll. If the phone rings and rings in your home in Newburyport and it is a friend or your son who cares you can get those messages when you get home. You didn't bring your cell phone you said.

I didn't I turned my old landline on.

Incredible. Good for you.

So you are here insulated from the mainland. Forget it all.

Molly looks at Weezie and thinks what a dear she is.

Well I've drunk enough. Tomorrow I'm going to Nantucket Safe Harbor for a dog to foster.

Oh Weezie how great.

What are you doing?

I think I'll take a tour it's been a few years.

Good idea. I'll stop by sometime tomorrow.

Okay. I'll get the check.

Weezie gives Molly a hug.

We're so lucky to be here.

Molly gathers her things.

Are you coming?

I'm staying.

Molly walks out of the Brotherhood.

WEEZIE'S CELL RINGS. Weezie answers it.

Hello.

Hi sis, it's Kathy.

Oh, hi. What's up?

Well we haven't talked for two months. Where are you? It's getting toward the season so I was wondering if you…just wondered…if you wanted to come visit over Christmas?

I'm not at the lake. I am on Nantucket.

That rich island?

Well it's the Christmas Stroll and you don't have to be rich to enjoy that.

Want company? I could take a few days off. See your darling nephew.

Oh I just sent him a sweater from a yarn shop here.

Nice. So you want company?

No I'm good really I am. Save the flight for somewhere else.

Yeah, like I'll take off work.

It's late here, Kathy, I'm wiped. Going to cut this short.

Oh, yeah right forgot.

Okay well let's talk on Christmas.

Sure, night. And thanks for calling.

Uh huh. Bye.

WEEZIE WALKS OUTSIDE. She sees Andrea crossing the street from Le Languedoc. Weezie crosses the street.

Hey.

Hey.

I'm just going home.

I just left thee a note. Would thee like to see the Meeting House tomorrow? Thee seemed interested when thee was in the shop.

Sure.

I'm going home too. Care to stop in for a cup of tea?

I'd love it.

Andrea and Weezie walk to Andrea's gate. After Andrea unlatched the front door and Weezie walked in Andrea could feel the weight of another human being inside her Mother's home.

Who was coming into Andrea's space? Andrea thought she had made a mistake inviting this stranger inside. Why did she blurt out those words? Caution veering away from her Quaker code.

Something flickers. The moon comes from behind a cloud of white. How comforting it is to stand here. The Christmas lights from all the houses, a true fairy land. Christmas coming. Dickens and holly and poinsettias and baking cookies.

Andrea points to the fireplace room.

Weezie nods and makes her way to a chair.

I'll make tea.

Weezie sinks deep. She cannot believe she is sitting in a beautiful Nantucket home and a Quaker woman is making her tea.

What are the sounds she hears? Is it a call of a lost bird in the night? What are the curtains saying? What is her own heart saying? She can hardly breathe and must get hold of herself. This feeling of out of time for her…not the very familiar with Maggie at the lake.

Andrea enters the room. Weezie feels her body spin. Andrea sets the tea down on a small table. Milk or lemon?

Lemon.

The beating wings of seagulls over the sea come into the room. They look away. They are strangers.

There is silence. Hesitancy.

The tea cups the tea hot to the tongue.

The fire burns moths to a flame...

Nothing can stay like this for long. Speech will ruin the silence yet it must come.

She cannot remember her past.

Does thee know Quakers?

No.

Would thee like to visit a Meeting with me?

Yes. Very much.

My note, oh thee is repeating, yes, the Meeting

House is open tomorrow afternoon.

I must go home, forgive me. I was drinking champagne with a friend earlier.

She finds one more ounce of vitality.

Do you mind all the strangers for the stroll? Like me?

Not at all. We must keep our stores open or we wouldn't make it through the winter.

Thank you for the tea. What time again? When would I meet you at the Meeting House?

Four would be fine.

Alright. Goodnight then.

Andrea walks Weezie to the front door.

Thee knows thy way home?

Yes. I do. ….

Good night.

Night.

IT IS SNOWING when Andrea opens the door. Weezie walks through the gate then stops and turns around for one last glance at this stranger.

Andrea closed the door and went back to the fire-light her tea and her old chair.

What had her conversion been like? She didn't want to follow her Mother into the faith but time and routine kept her so close to it all it suddenly crept in. Her Mother had raised her a Quaker. Though she never saw her Mother rise up at the Meeting and speak she knew she was allowed to if she was so moved.

Andrea had not been moved. She was of two minds now follow the heritage from her Mother or let it go. Her father had divorced her Mother over Quakerism.

Could she make a new start on the island? Everyone knew her as a devout Quaker.

What would her two best Quaker friends Betsy and Anne say to her about bringing a stranger into her home? It was just not done. Why bring a stranger into her home? A stranger with a funny name. She hadn't even asked Weezie what it stood for.

She could submit to God everyday. Would shop-keeping and saying hello and good-night to her customers and dinner alone be enough?

It was what she had prayed for years ago to hear a simple calling and do what God willed. He led her life to the Quaker community. She loved the Quaker community of the past and wished she could have lived then. Back when it was the faith of the island. Back when men were rich whalers and Mary Coffin Starbuck brought everyone to her lovely home for Meetings. She could weep and pray with every word brought to her from the traveling ministers. Now they were lucky to get a minister every week. The population of Quakers was down to twenty.

What a ridiculous way to be. Yet her Mother instilled the belief of the Light of the divine inside her and it felt like that very Light was her sextant across the moments and days and hours of her life on Nantucket. No clergy no liturgy no Bible just pay attention to God's wishes at the Meeting.

Who was doing any better? She did not like to compare herself with others. But she did give herself a moment of encouragement because she was living without evil. Why shouldn't she be proud? The world was nothing but evil now everywhere she looked. She heard news stories. Stabbings were all over the world. They had joined gun violence. Thank God no stabbings had come to Nantucket.

She was not going to be devoured by evil. It was not in her faith. No violence! No wars! No guns! Truth, what she knew from her Quaker upbringing, was never going to be in the world. But she could espouse those beliefs here on Nantucket.

People protesting in the streets? Military flights over the island? The great avenues of civilization and war were not going to happen here. She lived a life no one ever heard of off-island. It was not a thing that could be said in words One could weep one could sob one could crawl into a hole but the ocean kept moving around the island creating light in ripples and sparkles. There was peace here not the violence far away.

Now she was one of twenty kind solemn righteous Quakers with a divine Light so what was she doing with this stranger in her house? Andrea could not get this question out of her head and it kept her up way past her bedtime. Her thoughts felt like a shuttle back and forth across a loom.

She had to have another glass of wine to sleep. She had customers to take care of in the morning. She switched back to another glass of sherry.

When her mind did this the only thing that could calm her was climbing to the Widow's Walk. She would do just that. She climbed the narrow stairs to the roof holding a glass of sherry. The Widow's Walk hugged the sky and stars.

This is who she is: apron and slippers and broom and dustpan and washing and drying and ironing. Clean, it all must be clean. When everything is clean it feels closer to perfection and her own inner Light. How can anything rise to the divine when it is filled with filth and dirt and grime?

The stars show Orion's Belt and the Big Dipper and

Sirius. Oh the whalers and their sextants sailing all the way to the Pacific was beyond her imagination. She couldn't leave the island ever, never.

But tonight in the creamy full moon radiance something unknown, unexpected, seemed to be swirling around her deep inside the emotions of grief something else was stirring.

She lifted her head to the December sky and watched her breath go from her lungs to her mouth her eyes stung and then she hallucinated or imagined that big leviathan rising from the sea like all faithful Nantucketers could see a whale in their imagination one they never had to discuss with anyone because it was a private and collective feeling of whales and whalebones haunting everyone on the island for 300 years the burning oil smell could still float across the foggy morning from S'conset into town nothing distinguishable to the day's linear reality but underneath where dreams floated ghosts of whales were there under the sea ready to rise up from the imperceptible huge breath of the sea…

When Andrea climbed back downstairs she heard a knock at the door. She opened the latch. There was

Brad. Would she ask Brad in? Divorced with no kids. Just the opposite of Quaker. Loves his country music: Hank Garth Willie! He will hope she is in a Christmas Stroll jolly mood. How many nights had she let him walk away alone. She opened the door. He began to tell her about his day at station WCAI. She could always follow his words as he was simple in telling his stories. They had had talks before about Nantucket. They both kept a small radius around the island. She invited him in for a glass of sherry. They sat by the fire.

In moments she knew he wanted to be in her bed. She thought about lying under his arm snuggling like two peas in a pod. She knew her clean sheets would comfort both of them and the smells permeating her home of herbs and yarns and books and lavender and coffee sent him into ecstasy.

He would be there tomorrow. Their seventeen years now were good years of soft quiet Quaker flirting. She slept with him a few times. A slow penetrating softness that left her wide-eyed looking up at the ceiling unsatisfied while he snored away in his dreams. She often climbed to the Widow's Walk after those nights of flirting and sex. There looking out at the sea and stars she felt something bigger than flirting and sex. It made her soul soar.

She sent Brad home after one glass of sherry and made herself a pot of tea. She went back to the fire in the living room furnished with plain cotton and linen. Her Mother respected the plain habits of Quakers. Andrea's cup of tea went back three centuries when the whalers brought exotic teas back from China. She loved this time in the evening. She loved to hear the quiet of the island. And the warmth of the house around her that had nurtured her all these many years. Now this wooden building of grey shingles was hers alone.

Now she sat alone grieving. But others suffered too. All her Quaker friends had suffered a death.

Now the shadows had fallen in the room. Purple light bounced from the fire onto the linen curtains. She could see her shadow.

She wanted to laugh with someone. To converse with someone whose mind went down secret alleys. She would not leave the island so there was nowhere to go to find this person.

She thought it might be good to bring a friend over for supper sometime. She knew several of the Quaker women. Her Mother would not want her alone.

Tomorrow the faces at the stroll would continue one more day. Faces and faces some greedy some solemn some curious some bored, most a false jolly, touching everything in the shop and always wanting to know how it all began for her. Will they move here and raise sheep? They seem to think so. Bundles in their arms, kids with candy canes licking messy. What piece of yarn will be picked up and ruined?

Suddenly the fire spit out an ember. She looked into the shadows and remembered a face. The sweetness of the face runs down the walls of her mind. Did she say her name?

Who was this person? Many women Quaker friends. Shall we be friends? Foolishness…God-given gift is a man, particularly a Quaker man. She had been taught that...What does a woman do when the moon is full? Can she be young again…Oh god yes, please, just once…she was never young and in love. Let me be flung up and down by a man who could capture a whale at sea.

Oh to toss her religion aside and be active…to dance to hear music in a bar…anyone will do tonight. The young man at the donut shop. Smiles every time she gets her muffin. She sits there and watches him flirt with all his peers the young woman with the big loopy earrings and tattoos. Shadows. She is losing it. He is twenty-five years younger than she is. It isn't the way. Three hundred years ago she'd be shunned.

Never…it all passed me by…the shop…working next to Mother. Am impatient with solitude…like draperies around me nothing moves. All in its place. No TV. Will read more on the Quakers' fight against slavery. All is night. The fire goes out. Another day of stroll early tomorrow.

And yet half in dream half in consciousness one last thought three centuries ago it still sticks now not so there are laws all laws of the church what church

All churches what is thee talking about not sure who was this woman with the blue coyote eyes in thee's home

Sleep was what she needed

And yet

WEEZIE WALKED BACK TO LE LANGUEDOC and up the stairs. She took the note from the doorway. She read Andrea's note.

Would thee like to see the Quaker Meeting House 4 p.m. tomorrow? Will meet thee there.

Weezie showered and crawled into bed with a Nancy Thayer book. She had three good things to think about — a puppy, a studio in Surfside and meeting Andrea. What would keep her from sleeping like a child tonight? Nothing. She wrapped herself in a cocoon and pulled the quilt up to her chin.

Weezie could hear a dog barking. She slept that night as if she were drunk.

MOLLY LEFT THE BROTHERHOOD and walked outside to hail a cab. She knew they would be working late due to strollers partying.

Island Cab came right away. She told him to take her to Monomoy Charles Rivers' home. It was close to ten o'clock. While she sat in the back seat she began to go over how she knew Weezie. She was a good friend, loyal always there for a good talk and they had so many shared experiences from their past.

It all started at the University of Pittsburgh when she went into nursing and Weezie took video production courses. But she grew bored making videos for insurance companies. It was gutsy to open the café with her friend Maggie at that lake in New York.

How mysterious they both were here for the stroll and yet neither had told the other. There were gaps in all good friendships.

And now Molly was on her way to Charles's home in Monomoy. How amazing life could be some days. There were surprises that could lead to new actions and decisions. She was ready for the mystery and the surprises. Molly was ready for life.

Molly opened her purse. She picked out a lovely piece of Mistletoe and smiled. This was going to be the first thing she did when she got to Charles's home. She would attach the Mistletoe to a doorway and push him over in the wheelchair. Then she would be forward and bend down to his lips and kiss him. It was such a tradition she knew he would not mind. But would he like it with her? She knew she was going to enjoy it with her whole heart. Her lips would tingle. There was something about him in the tavern when she first met him. Tonight that first kiss was coming into that zone of real after years as an abstract desire. What fantasies did she have with him? What would he imagine with her? Or would he keep it all to himself? She put the Mistletoe back in her purse. The cab pulled into the driveway.

Police cars were parked in the circular driveway.

She got out of the cab.

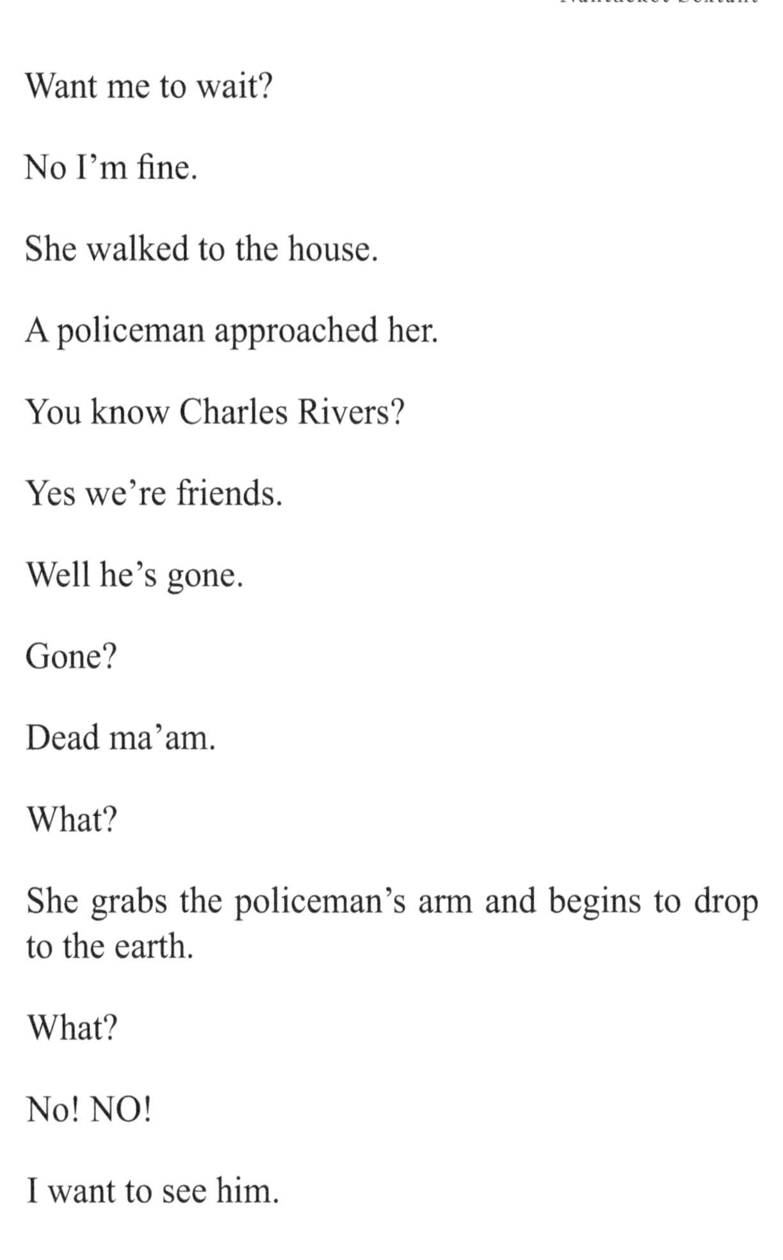

Want me to wait?

No I'm fine.

She walked to the house.

A policeman approached her.

You know Charles Rivers?

Yes we're friends.

Well he's gone.

Gone?

Dead ma'am.

What?

She grabs the policeman's arm and begins to drop to the earth.

What?

No! NO!

I want to see him.

He's not here. He had a massive heart attack this evening around 9.

The policeman watched her face and tried to lift her up.

Molly sank to the ground.

Please, let me sit here.

The officer walked back to the patrol cars. He kept watching Molly.

She was out of earshot now. Her heart sounded like a tidal wave thump thump thump thump!

She knew the signs of grief and more grief inside her head. It took over every cosmic moment lived and unlived. It gutted. She nearly lost all sight of the man who she knew so little about. What was his boyhood like? She would never know. Why did his marriage break up? What were his dreams? Did he want to make love to her?

Molly could barely move her arms and legs.

The policeman came back.

Here let me take you home.

He lifted her up.

She held on tight.

I'm…I'm at…

Where you staying?

The Periwinkle.

I'll take you there.

Yes.

When she got to her room she laid on the bed and sobbed.

THE NEXT MORNING MOLLY packed her bags.

She was leaving. Since she had no phone on her she left Weezie a note on her door.

That morning Weezie was picking out a foster dog.

Molly walked to Steamboat Wharf and walked up the ramp to the ferry.

She had failed. She thought life could change but it couldn't. She was stuck in her past memories and nothing could pull her from it. She would resume her life…all of it. It wouldn't be hard. It was routine and she knew it well.

Not even her beloved Nantucket could take her away from her known…I am this…I am that. Charles had sunk to the bottom like the goldfish in his backyard pond that froze one winter. Ronny had told her about the fish. Charles was dead the sweet man who flirted with her in the tavern in Charlestown now gone.

How could life be so strange so cruel so impermanent? To dash her wishes and hopes and the courage it took to even entertain another relationship with another human being now lost forever.

She would not attend the funeral she was already on the ferry.

It had all failed. Those schoolgirl dreams of another romance with this man from Charlestown. She could hear herself asking that it not be true the old chestnut of bargaining in the face of death…if God you bring him back…then I will…will what?

He wasn't old only sixty. Would have been so wonderful to flirt with him and to finally make it into his bed and the loving they could have done.

Rolling toward and on and over each other's bodies with all the newness of life in another act but those Act Two articles were not true, they hadn't worked for Molly. She would never read another one of those self-help articles again!

She had tried and failed. There would be no new aim or ambition or trying ever again. She could rest now and do nothing. She would accept the failure of a new life on Nantucket.

She would give herself the decency of looking at her past...the rest of her life and think that she would not change a thing about it if she could live it again. She would do it all over again the same way.

She had not gone to Nantucket in any previous years to live permanently, had she? No. She'd harbored all those fears about the food not coming over to the island about snow blocking the harbor for days and about the electrical power going off and what then?

Who would look in on her when she knew no one? The ferry sped for Hyannis.

She would not have to worry about any of it now.

Back to her own familiar worries in Newburyport full of anxiety about who might help her get to a hospital if she broke a leg. Or if she felt dizzy like she did in March. She would never go off again in the car and cause herself another accident.

The joke was on her.

Back to what she knew.

Which was so small now and she would end up in some nursing home because her son would not come from California and take care of her.

Yes, she would end up in some nursing home alone now. After the sparkling dream of living with Charles in his beautiful house in Monomoy on the island of Nantucket.

My god!

Get me off this ferry get me back home so I can take care of this wound of the heart. She pulled her compact from her purse and looked at a face she could barely remember.

EARLY MORNING WEEZIE stopped at Safe Harbor for Animals. She spoke with a woman and told her she was there to foster a dog for a month.

The woman led her to a room where a few dogs and puppies were roaming around. Weezie stood still.

After a few minutes a young mutt came up to her ankles and put his white paws there.

Weezie bent down and pet him.

Yes, I'll take him.

She put him in the Jeep and went to the Surfside studio. She had moved her things very early that morning.

When she went back to check out Weezie saw a note from Molly.

Oh my god. And I cannot call her on her cell phone, she doesn't have it with her.

Weezie looked up Molly's landline number and dialed.

I just read your note. You must be in shock, Molly, I'm sorry very, very sad picked message up…I didn't know him but heard your excitement about getting to know him if there is anything I can do here let me know and take care of yourself…Call me when you feel like it…I am staying for the month and found a great puppy this morning…Molly take care of your-self, so sorry.

Weezie knew the call didn't help so she hung up.

She climbed in the Jeep and hugged her new puppy.

What will I call you for a month?

Tigger.

Yeah Tigger, like in Pooh, you're a jumper.

The puppy wagged his tail.

Weezie loved her puppy and suddenly loved her whole life. She was happy she'd had a friend like Maggie all those years and now she was healing on

Nantucket. She walked outside with Tigger in the woods and moors near the studio. She saw a bush full of holly so she broke off a tiny branch to put in her studio. She leaped like Tigger. Life was good again. It had some undefinable mystery to it. She could feel empathy for Molly but there was another part of her that was bright and clear again and she wanted to rejoice in it. She walked as if she belonged to the land underneath her feet. She raised her arms to the sky. She was alive again.

And there might even be some mystery to it all. Would she be friends with Andrea? She felt free for the first time in her life. Her lungs filled with sea air and her heart filled with the stroll. There was Tigger standing by her legs.

Weezie looked down at her legs which were bare from calf to ankle in her Capris. There was a small round tick on her leg.

Oh god! She'd gone and ignored the one precaution about ticks: stay away from edges of gardens and trees and shady spots. She walked in a shady garden and near moor grasses and trees. It was the black leg tick.

Oh God.

She scooped Tigger up in her arms and ran to the studio.

She examined Tigger. All clear then she looked at her legs and saw one hiding on her sock against her skin.

God, no.

She left Tigger with a treat and jumped into her Jeep on her way to the ER at the Cottage Hospital. Dr. Lamy trained his staff to deal with ticks as there were far too many deer on the island. A nurse gave her medicine and a shot and she was on her way back home to rest. She knew she would be uncomfortable for a few days but it was not life-threatening.

She slept the day away. Never once did she know it was 4 o'clock. The medicine was working on the tick and Weezie's mind. She drifted away.

ANDREA LOVED SITTING OUTSIDE EARLY in the little garden looking at the holly plants in the mild December sun. The sun washed away her night of chaos and restless sleep. She knows she remained a Quaker because they kept her from the crazy world outside. The acceleration and craziness she sensed off-island was nothing she wanted to ever endure. Cities were not her cup of tea.

She wanted the island but figuring out her own spiritual needs was always puzzling. She knew she should take up a hobby like painting or photography. Maybe photography. Tim, a photographer, would be happy to help her start with an old Nikon or Canon.

With her Mother gone she had stopped ironing so many clothes. She kept one gray dress to wear to Meeting but not five like she used to do. She had enough furniture. It was a pleasant home on Fair Street and not far from the Quaker Meeting House.

She did love to wander into the Maria Mitchell

Observatory and look out at the stars at night. Astronomy now that was a calling. She did not have a calling. She wondered why? Life had been structured from the time she was sent to Quaker school. She never felt her own mind soar. What would that feel like?

The island could be depended upon to change into its magnificent seasons and it comforted her. The sea around the harbor tossed its spray every time she went down to the docks. She rarely went to the big beaches like Surfside and S'conset and Nobadeer where the young people sun tanned, noisy, surfed. She looked at the sky always ready to see stars. Perhaps she would take a book out from the Mitchell Museum and study the stars at least enough to name. Perhaps she would look at a sextant.

Andrea enjoyed cooking about four times a week. The other nights she ordered a pizza or wrap. Three days a week after running the yarn shop she would stop in the library and visit the children's area. She would read to children whenever she could. It satisfied her need for children in a safe environment.

Nantucket was her love. She could walk its

cobblestone streets and look at the fine architecture the Quakers had built the rest of her life. Maybe someday a new thought or two would come but for now she was settled and only the lack of spirit in the Meetings filled her thoughts.

Brad walked in the little gate.

Anyone home?

Yes, good morning Brad, come in.

Brad walked in with his Irish Setter.

How strange to be combined with another to be mixed up out of one's solitude.

Would thee like some bread and jam and tea?

Sure, thanks, Andrea. Just out walking with Red.

Oh he's a beautiful dog. How old is he now?

Seven and still frisky.

Andrea pets Red's head. She hands Brad the sandwich.

Please sit thee down.

Thank you.

Brad sits down. Red sprawls down by his feet.

You still have a few roses.

Yes isn't it heavenly?

They both look at the holly.

The bells ring at the Unitarian Church. Seven. They sit. She knows he wants to console her. His jacket collar blows in the breeze. Sitting with Brad is comforting. But not the way he desires.

He touches a spot on his cheek where he nicked himself shaving. Shaving and shaving every day. He is not a beard man though that makes him odd now. He supposes if he lived here 300 years before he might have a beard. The world is moving quickly past him this year he can feel it. Time has dropped and left him feeling old. Now the movement of the world will invade the island in the Christmas season and he will hide in his cubicle announcing every busy moment of it all to the thousands of bodies swirling in the latitude longitude of Nantucket all strangers that will invade his island home. A great life festival surrounds him...as good as the Greek festivals of old he thinks. His body feels desire mounting whenever he looks at Andrea. She being so calm and stalwart. *Hells bells she looks good.* He examines his conscience. He does nothing only the shadow of a man. He wants to touch that thick hair that flows around her face and ears so fragrant he nearly swoons like a girl when she brushes by him with the tea cup.

And here he is again in this garden with Andrea, this unknown moment growing longer and longer with the silence. And what if one day he did not come over for the early breakfast. Would she miss him? Should he announce his intentions of asking her to marry him? Probably not. Would he find another if she said 'no'? He will not ask her. He will not be rejected. He is weak and like a cat in his habits.

Thank thee for announcing Yarn Pastures the first day.

Of course. He finishes his sandwich. Red looks up at him.

Must be going Red needs his breakfast too.

If you need anything, Andrea.

Andrea nods.

He stands up and walks out with Red.

AT THE QUAKER MEETING HOUSE Andrea rises from her bench. The congregation sits in silence.

Thee will hear me now. Thee my devoted Quakers here on this island where we can still hear the sounds of our women weeping for the husbands brothers fathers and sons thee have lost at sea to the whale and storm and weak broken whaleboats

Hear thy sound when a divine Light rises upward from thee

And let thee say what has been in thee mind in thee heart

The land is what we love can you hear that divine sentiment thee can love no other for it is thee land where thee and thou have lived and breathed and loved and worked and birthed and died

We cannot mourn any longer thou seekers to

other places: to Sandwich and New Bedford and Philadelphia and Nova Scotia and the Carolinas. Thou are Quakers of Nantucket. Thou has the long ago past, resplendent in virtue and Light and non-violence. Our dear forebears and faithful founder Mary Coffin Starbuck who weeped in her Parliament House when the words of thy minister moved her to tears; when thee heard the Truth the everlasting Creator's gift

Truth for thy lives and ways

Truth and more Truth with no need to hear the liturgy or the Bible, thee does not have to evangelize about Jesus; Jesus is another story for another time; thou knows this…thou feels this inside

In the vitality of the other years and cultures Quaker Truth and Light were all thee needed

We are the Truth now in our hearts and our divine spirit keeps us here forever

No other way can lead thee; thee will not take up GUNS and VIOLENCE and WARS that rage around us…Thee did not start wars…Thee did not stab to death a young female Israeli soldier; thee did not stab a mother and child Christmas shopping in Dublin; thee did not stab a famous author during a presentation on stage. The stabbings and gun violence will go on and on and thee will have no part of it

Thee will stay within the divine Light thee will respect the young who will bring us hope and new ministers

Thee is used to the wider world for it was our captains on whaling ships that brought thee our teas and silks and spices and forged the way of knowing what is beyond our shores. Thee are still open to the world in peace and thee will continue to show a worthy face

Thee's spirits keep thee here and thee's spirits speak from thee heart

That to know the Truth and to remain here on Nantucket is thee's

divine path

Thank thee

Andrea sits down. She takes a deep breath. She knows she will stay on Nantucket no matter how few Quakers there are at the Meetings. She didn't cause all the schisms of the past 300 years! Nantucket is her heritage! Her livelihood! Her memory!

One does not throw away all of this because the world does not want the Society of Friends. The world wants to do nothing but wrangle with thee.

A woman must cherish and guard who she is and has become.

When the Meeting is finished Andrea walks outside.

Weezie is standing there.

Thee spoke for the first time. Thee never dared before.

May I walk with you? Her eyes level on Andrea's face.

O, thee is going to the Quaker cemetery.

I've never been.

Andrea links her arm with Weezie's. They reach the

cemetery and walk to her Mother's unmarked grave.

May I apologize for not coming yesterday at 4?

Thee does not know me well enough for an apology.

There is a silent moment.

Mother lies here.

No headstones?

Back to the earth and sand.

Weezie nods.

They stand together without speaking. Seagulls flap overhead. A foghorn sounds in the harbor.

The sun creeps over the land and the waves beat along every inch of the beaches. Strands of seaweed toss about in the high tide.

Silence lingers.

They can see in each other's eyes that Truth is with them. They are both whole persons.

A spirit will embrace them as women were embraced for the past 300 years on Nantucket.

They will go to each other's home for tea and supper and social chats.

Andrea will keep her shop Yarn Pastures as her Mother taught her and she will sit by the fireside at night and drink her tea.

Weezie will keep Tigger for more than a month. She will talk to the owner of the Surfside studio and get a deal for the winter. She will figure it out after that. She knows she will volunteer at the Weezie Children's library. Synchronicity.

The following week Weezie calls Molly.

I won't come visit again, that's for sure. The whole experience taught me I am not a badass woman able to change.

Weezie hears the pain.

It is what it is, she informs Weezie over and over.

WEEZIE OFTEN STOOD OUTSIDE Andrea's shop on her way home in the dark.

In those December moments Weezie's thoughts seemed to swirl as if she were in a lovely dream when the tree branches above her head shook snow

the sky filled with stars

darkness covered the streets and alleys

and darkening waves crested on the beaches

The world was quiet now

Snow kept falling from the sky

Weezie opened her mouth to catch snowflakes on her tongue and then they melted

Her soul rose up and she heard her favorite James Joyce quote from ***The Dead:***

Yes, the newspapers were right: snow was general all over...It lay thickly drifted on the crooked crosses and headstones, on the spears of the little gate, on the barren thorns...snow falling faintly through the universe and faintly falling, like the descent of their last end, upon all the living and the dead

Weezie closed her eyes again

snowflakes touched her tongue...and hair and face

OVER ON MILK STREET at the MMA Observatory the December stars sparkled…

a sextant stood ready to measure angular distances of celestial bodies spinning…

latitude… 41° 17' 0. 46" N

longitude... 70° 5' 58.06" W

Yes, snow fell silently upon the moors

and

cemeteries of Nantucket

Printed in the USA
CPSIA information can be obtained
at www.ICGtesting.com
CBHW022158110424
6799CB00015B/114